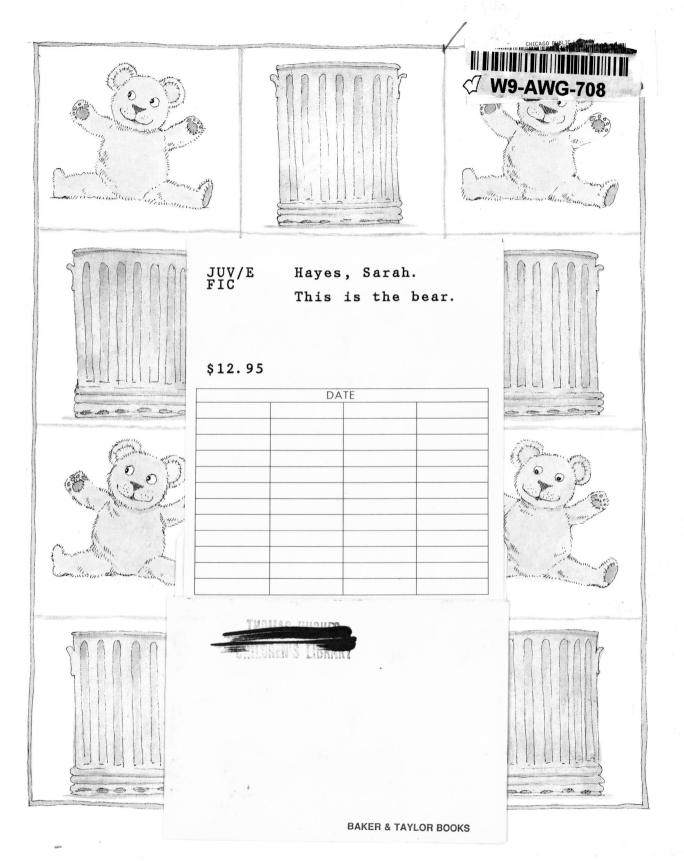

CHICAGO PUBLIC
W9-AWG-708

JUV/E
FIC

Hayes, Sarah.

This is the bear.

$12.95

| DATE | | | |
|---|---|---|---|
| | | | |
| | | | |
| | | | |
| | | | |
| | | | |
| | | | |
| | | | |
| | | | |
| | | | |
| | | | |
| | | | |
| | | | |

THOMAS HUGHES
CHILDREN'S LIBRARY

BAKER & TAYLOR BOOKS

*For Barbara, who makes bears*
S.H.

*For Edward (Teddy) Craig*
H.C.

Text copyright © 1986 by Sarah Hayes
Illustrations copyright © 1986 by Helen Craig

All rights reserved.

Second U.S. edition 1993
First published in Great Britain in 1986 by Walker Books Ltd., London.

*Library of Congress Cataloging-in-Publication Data:*

Hayes, Sarah
This is the bear / written by Sarah Hayes : illustrated
by Helen Craig.—2nd U.S. ed.
Summary: A toy bear is accidentally taken to the dump,
but is rescued by a boy and a dog.
[1. Teddy bears—Fiction. 2. Stories in rhyme.]
I. Craig, Helen, ill. II. Title.
PZ8.3.H324Th   1993                    92-53421
[E]—dc20

ISBN 1-56402-189-0

10 9 8 7 6 5 4 3 2 1

Printed in Hong Kong

The pictures for this book were done in watercolor and ink.

Candlewick Press
2067 Massachusetts Avenue
Cambridge, Massachusetts 02140

# — THIS IS THE —
# BEAR

by
Sarah Hayes

illustrated by
Helen Craig

R0090633801

CANDLEWICK PRESS
CAMBRIDGE, MASSACHUSETTS

This is the bear
who fell in the bin.

This is the dog
who pushed him in.

This is the man
who picked up the sack.

This is the driver
who would not come back.

This is the bear
who went to the dump

and fell on the pile
with a bit of a bump.

This is the boy
who took the bus

and went to the dump

to make a fuss.

# This is the man
# in an awful grump

who searched
and searched
and searched the dump.

# This is the bear
# all cold and cross

who never thought
he was really lost.

This is the dog

who smelled the smell

of a bone

and a can

and a bear as well.

This is the man
who drove them home –

the boy, the bear,
and the dog with a bone.

This is the bear

neat as a pin

who would not say
just where he had been.

This is the boy
who knew quite well,

but promised his friend

he would not tell.

And this is the boy
who woke up in the night
and asked the bear
if he felt all right —
and was very surprised
when the bear gave a shout,
"How soon can we have
another day out?"

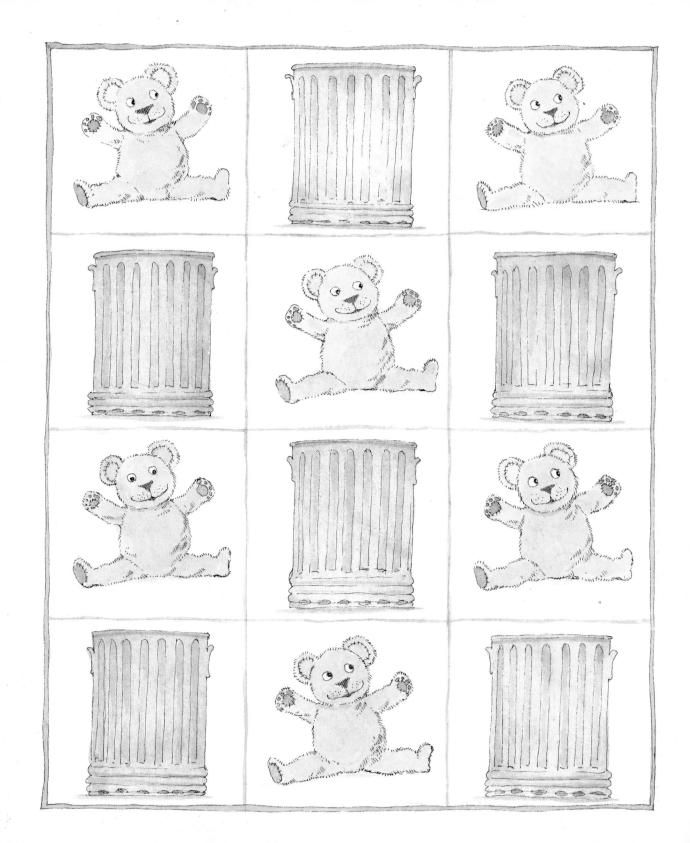